If I Had a Tail

Written by
Jane Clarke

Illustrated by
Jan Dolby

If I had a tail like a cat,

I would curl up on a mat.

If I had a tail like a kangaroo,

I would hop away with you.

I would swing from tree to tree,

if I had a tail like a chimpanzee.

If I had a fin for a tail,

I would play with a whale.

Would you like the sound I make,

if I had a tail like a rattlesnake?

I would fly up to the sky,

if I had a tail like a noisy magpie.

Would you like a tail like me?

If you had a tail, what would it be?